HITLER'S
DAUGHTER

HITLER'S DAUGHTER

BY JACKIE FRENCH

HARPERCOLLINS*PUBLISHERS*

Library of Congress Cataloging-in-Publication Data

French, Jackie.

Hitler's daughter / by Jackie French.

p.   cm.

Summary: After hearing a fictional tale about Hitler's daughter, Mark wonders what it would
be like if someone he loved and trusted turned out to be evil.

ISBN 0-06-008652-1 — ISBN 0-06-008653-X (lib. bdg.)

1. Hitler, Adolf, 1889-1945—Family—Juvenile fiction. [1. Hitler, Adolf, 1889-1945—
Family—Fiction. 2. Storytelling—Fiction. 3. Australia—Fiction.] I. Title.

PZ7 .F88903Hi 2003

[Fic]—dc21

2002014459

Originally published in 1999 in Australia by Angus & Robertson
An Imprint of HarperCollins*Publishers*
25 Ryde Road, Pymble, Sydney, NSW 2073, Australia

3 4 5 6 7 8 9 10

❖

First U.S. edition, 2003

HITLER'S
DAUGHTER

ONE

IT WAS RAINING the day that Mark first heard about Hitler's daughter. The cows in Harrison's paddock were wet and brown and mournful. Raindrops dripped down their noses as they huddled with their backs to the wind.

There was nothing in the world quite as sad-looking as wet cows, thought Mark as he hauled his damp schoolbag further into the bus shelter. Do cows ever get colds? he wondered. What would happen if they sneezed?

The Wallaby Creek Progress Association had built the bus shelter last year. It was made of curved yellow tin— easily big enough for the four kids who caught the bus at this corner.

The idea had been to keep the kids out of the wind and rain while they waited for the bus. In Mark's opinion the whole idea was a flop.

Before the bus shelter was built he sat in the car with

1

Mum when it rained, dry and warm with the heater going till the bus trundled around the corner. And everyone else sat in their cars too.

Ever since the shelter had been finished Mum just dropped him off with a kiss and a wave and hurried back to the warm kitchen at home till it was time for her to leave for her job at the stock-and-station agent's in town, leaving him in the damp, cold bus shelter with fingers of rainwater tickling down his neck.

Mark usually got to the bus stop first. Mum was early for *everything*, thought Mark dismally, pulling his jacket closer around his shoulders. She always left enough time to have a flat tire *and* go back if Mark forgot his homework *and* fill in any note he'd forgotten to give her last night and just remembered at the bus stop, as well as—

"Hey, move your bag!" Ben said as he shoved it out of his way and dashed under the shelter. "Did you see the creek? It's gone all yellow. The bridge'll go if this keeps up," he added hopefully.

Ben lived on the other side of the paddock. It took about two minutes for him to race between the cow droppings to the bus shelter.

"Hey, have you ever noticed that cows look all shiny when they're wet?" asked Mark.

2

"No," said Ben. He shoved the hood on his parka back.

"Like someone's polished them."

"Who cares?" Ben scraped his boot heels across the concrete floor to get rid of the mud. "Hey, there's Anna."

"Her mum must have picked up Little Tracey too," said Mark.

Anna dashed from the car, her bag clutched close to try and protect it from the rain. Little Tracey stomped through the puddles.

Little Tracey had been "Little" since her first day on the bus. (Big Tracey got on two stops later.) Little Tracey *was* little, thought Mark. He wondered if she'd always be little—like Mum's fox terrier, which would grow into an ankle-biter no matter how old it was.

"Hi," said Anna, dumping her bag in the shelter.

"Hi," said Mark. "Hey, Anna, have you ever heard a cow sneeze?"

Anna considered the question. "No," she admitted.

Little Tracey shoved her bag under the seat and plunked herself down beside the others. She wore yellow boots, splattered with orange clay. "Anna says we can play the Game!" she announced.

Ben shrugged, and went back to scraping the mud off

his boots. "I don't mind," he said.

"Alright," said Mark obligingly. The Game was okay, and, anyway, there wasn't anything else to do till the bus came.

The Game had started last year on Little Tracey's second day at school. She had cried, with great deep sniffs and her eyes widened as though that could keep the tears away.

Anna had grabbed Little Tracey's hand and hauled her into the bus shelter and announced, "Let's play a game."

Little Tracey had sniffed back more tears.

"What sort of game?" Mark had asked. He'd hoped it wasn't going to be I Spy or something dumb like that.

"The Story Game," Anna had said. "I used to play it with my grandma."

Little Tracey had looked up enquiringly at Anna, blinking her wet eyelashes.

"You make up a character," Anna had said to Little Tracey, "and I'll make up a story about them."

Mark had thought it sounded boring, but Little Tracey had sat still, quietly sniffling, so, to be helpful, Mark had said, "Okay. How about a story about a . . . a . . . an alien who comes to earth . . ."

Anna had shaken her head. "It's Tracey's story," she'd said. "What do you want a story about, Tracey?"

Little Tracey had just sniffled.

"How about a fish?" Mark had suggested helpfully. "Or a whale or a mermaid or a . . ." He'd hesitated. What were little kids interested in?

"A horse," Little Tracey had whispered suddenly. "I want a story about a horse."

Anna had grinned. "Okay," she'd said. "What's the horse's name?"

"Socks," Little Tracey had said. "And he's got a baby brother called . . . called Buttons and he lives in a paddock with his mum and dad and . . ."

That was the beginning of the Game.

They'd played the Game every day for a week until Little Tracey got used to the bus and school, and then they played it just for a treat on her birthday, or when it rained and you couldn't leave the bus shelter to play catch, and the wind was biting at your ankles.

The rain gurgled down the gutter, hiccuped at a bit of rock, then sped down and around the corner to the creek. A cow mooed sadly across the wet grass. "Okay, what do you want the story to be about?" Mark asked.

"I want a story about . . . about a fairy," said Little

5

Tracey, drumming her muddy heels on her schoolbag.

Ben groaned. "How about something good—like a gangster? Hey, how about a gangster who steals a million dollars and . . ."

"How about a dinosaur?" suggested Mark.

"A baby one," agreed Tracey eagerly. "A baby dinosaur called Billie and she gets separated from her mother and . . ."

"Ugh!" snorted Ben rudely.

"I'll choose this time," said Anna suddenly.

Mark stared. "But you never choose."

Anna shrugged. "Then it's my turn, isn't it?"

"Just choose something decent," said Ben. "No fairies or goldfish like the last time."

"I'm getting another goldfish next time we go to town," said Tracey. "It's going to be black and red and . . ."

"How can you have a black-and-red goldfish?" demanded Ben. "That's dumb."

"The bus'll be here if you don't shut up," said Mark. "Go on, Anna. What's the story going to be about?"

Anna hesitated. "It's . . . it's about Hitler's daughter," she announced.

"Hey cool," said Ben.

"Who's Hitler?" demanded Little Tracey.

"He was this guy in World War Two," explained Ben. "He was the leader of Germany—they were the enemy in the war. Well, Japan was too. But Hitler had all these Brownshirts and the Gestapo and they tortured people and had concentration camps and things like that and everyone had to go '*Sieg heil!*' or '*Heil Hitler!*' You know, like in those movies on TV."

"But Hitler didn't have a daughter," protested Mark.

"Who cares?" said Ben. "Hitler's better than fairies and goldfish. Maybe she was a fighter pilot like the Red Baron! No, that was World War One, wasn't it?"

"But . . ." objected Mark. He tried to explain. "But we can't have a story about something that's not real."

"Why not?" demanded Ben. "Fairies aren't real, are they?"

"No, of course not. But . . ."

"They are *too* real," interrupted Little Tracey.

"But . . ." Mark stopped. It *did* seem different somehow to make up stuff about a real person. But there was no way he could put his feeling into words. "Okay then," he said finally. "What was her name?"

"Valdimara," said Ben with glee.

"You got that from TV last night," objected Mark.

"You know, that Vampire Princess thing."

"So what?"

"You can't have someone from TV in the Game. Anyway, Valdiwhatsit isn't German."

"Austrian," said Anna softly. "Hitler was Austrian."

"What's the difference?" said Ben, irritated. "Who knows any Austrian names anyway?"

"Her name was Heidi," stated Little Tracey.

"But that's from that sappy book . . ."

"Oh, for Pete's sake, what does it matter?" demanded Mark. "The bus'll be here soon. Go on, Anna. Her name was Heidi and she was Hitler's daughter."

"And she lived in a castle," decided Little Tracey.

"It wasn't really like a castle," said Anna slowly. "But it was big, with wide terraces, and so many rooms that . . . that Heidi could never count them all."

Mark settled back on the seat. It always took a while for Anna to settle in to a story. But it was pretty good when she did. She always added details so you saw the story in your mind.

"There were Fräulein Gelber's rooms, which smelled of cigarettes. Fräulein Gelber wasn't supposed to smoke. Duffi said that smoking gave you cancer. But Heidi knew Fräulein Gelber smoked anyway.

"The kitchen smelled of flour: cold flour in the sacks, and hot flour in the oven, and even spilled flour had a different smell, though when Heidi told Fräulein Gelber she just laughed.

"There were the 'don't go down there' rooms, where Duffi talked with people in uniforms and flowery dresses . . ."

"Who was Duffi?" demanded Ben.

"Hitler," said Anna. "I don't know why she called him Duffi. I don't even know if it means anything. It was just what she did."

Ben sniffed. "Dumb," he said. "Go on then. Get to the good part."

"Duffi's own rooms were upstairs, but she was never to go there either. When Duffi visited he came to her rooms instead."

Little Tracey bounced on the seat. "What were Heidi's rooms like?"

"I'm not sure," said Anna.

"I know," said Little Tracey. "They were really, really big, and everything was pink, and she had one of those beds with curtains and it was pink as well, and all of one wall was a TV and . . ."

"They didn't have TV then," objected Mark.

"Who cares?" said Ben. "It's just a story. Go on, Anna. Get to the battles."

"The battles?"

"Yeah, you know. The good stuff. The Russian front and Rommel in Egypt and the V2 rockets . . ."

"How do you know all this?" demanded Mark.

"I did a project last term, dummy. It's cool. Go on, Anna. How about she goes to Egypt with Rommel and drives a tank through the Sahara Desert? Or flies a Messerschmidt—that'd be even better."

Anna fiddled with the zipper on her parka. "I don't know about Messerschmidts—or about any of the battles. Look, this isn't going to work. Hitler's daughter was a silly idea. Forget I started it, okay? How about another story? Tracey, you can choose."

"I want a story about Heidi," said Little Tracey.

"Okay," said Anna hurriedly. "Let's make her a princess. Princess Heidi . . ."

"No," said Little Tracey stubbornly. "I want a story about the other Heidi. The one you were talking about."

"Oh, alright then. But I can't tell you about battles. She never saw any battles."

"She must have!" declared Ben. "She was Hitler's daughter!"

Anna shook her head. "He kept her away from all the battles. He kept her away from everyone. No one knew he had ever been married, and no one knew about Heidi. She lived with Fräulein Gelber at Berchtesgaden—that was where Hitler had a house in the country and that was the only world she knew."

"But why?" insisted Mark. "Why did he keep her secret?"

"What does it matter?" asked Ben. "It's just a story anyway."

"Because she had a birthmark," said Anna softly. "A great red blotch across her face. And one of her legs was shorter than the other, so she limped . . . just a little bit.

"But Hitler wanted to breed a perfect race—the Aryan race, it was called. Children with blue eyes and blond hair, tall children who could run and jump and conquer the world. But his daughter was small like him, and dark, and her face was marked like an iron had burnt across it, and she limped."

"Then he didn't love her." Little Tracey's voice was very small.

"Of course not," said Mark. "He was Hitler. I bet Hitler never loved anyone."

"I don't know if he loved her or not," said Anna. "She

always hoped he did."

"But someone like Hitler couldn't . . ." began Mark.

"Hey, here's the bus!" Ben jumped to his feet. "That story's weird . . ."

"I said it wasn't working," said Anna defensively.

"It's not weird! I like it!" insisted Little Tracey.

The bus screeched to a stop in front of them, splashing water on all sides.

"Thought you'd have melted in the rain by now," called old Mrs. Latter. She wore her green hat like a tea-cozy this morning, pulled right down over her salt-and-pepper ponytail, and she had on her green boots with a crack on one heel. "Sorry I'm late. Any of you listen to that stuff the Prime Minister said on the news this morning?"

No one had.

Mrs. Latter sighed. She liked a good argument about the news, which was why the bus was always late—she wanted to stop and argue about it with her husband.

"Come on, hop on then," she said.

Little Tracey scrambled onto the bus first, like she always did, and bounced into the front seat behind Mrs. Latter. Mark ambled behind Anna, with Ben following on his heels.

The bus lurched out from the side of the road, and began to wind its way between the paddocks.

"Anna?"

Anna turned around. "Yeah. What?"

"What happened to Heidi's mum?"

"I think she died," said Anna. "She must've died. Heidi never knew her."

"Oh," said Mark. He hesitated. "Anna?"

"Yes?" Anna craned her head around again.

"Will you go on with the story tomorrow?"

"Yes . . . No. If it's raining maybe. I thought you didn't like it."

"It's alright," said Mark.

TWO

SOMETHING WAS WRONG. Unfinished. It bothered him all the way through school.

It was Anna's story, of course. That's what was wrong. She wasn't telling it properly, not like it should be told.

Because somehow Mark knew that the story was *there*, in Anna's mind. She shouldn't have let them butt in. It was almost like she didn't want to tell it at all.

It shouldn't have mattered, of course. It was just one of Anna's stories, like the one about the goldfish that swam to Tasmania or the wild horses that took over the school or the secret gold mine under the butcher's shop.

But somehow Heidi had become real . . . no, she wasn't real, not yet. It was as though she *might* be real, if Anna just told them more.

And suddenly Mark wanted more than anything to know more.

The buses lined the road next to the school. When

he'd been small, Mark had thought they looked like lions waiting to swallow you and then burp you out at your bus stop.

Mark sat with Bonzo, as he always did, in the seat behind Anna and Big Traccy. Little Tracey sat with a kid almost as small as her. Ben sat in the backseat with his friends.

One by one all the other kids got off. Little Tracey's friend first, and Ben's friends and Bonzo at the stop by the store, then finally Big Tracey at Dirty Butter Creek.

Mark leaned forward and tapped Anna on the shoulder. "Hey, guess what?" he said.

"What?"

"I just worked out why it's called Dirty Butter Creek. I used to think there must have been a dairy or something here."

"Wasn't there?"

"No. I asked Dad once and he said there weren't any dairies around here. Just look at it now." Mark gazed down into the swirling yellow water.

"Hey, I see . . ." cried Anna. "It looks just like dirty butter, doesn't it? Yuck . . . all yellow and brown."

"Yeah. Anna, will you go on with the story tomorrow?"

"I don't know," said Anna slowly.

"Please."

"If you really want me to," said Anna, even more slowly.

"Yeah, I do," said Mark. "Look . . . how about getting down to the bus stop a bit earlier tomorrow, so you've got more time. I'll ask Mum, and your mum can pick up Little Tracey, say, fifteen minutes earlier."

"Oh, alright. I'll say we need to talk about a project for school."

"Thanks," said Mark. He leaned back in his seat again, then changed his mind and tapped her arm again.

"Anna."

"Yes."

"*You* tell the story tomorrow. I mean without us interrupting."

"What about Ben? Are you going to ask him to come early too?"

"You can get the story going before he gets there." Somehow he knew the story wouldn't go right if Ben were there.

THREE

THE RAIN GURGLED along the gutter and into the tank outside the kitchen window. The creek groaned and rumbled, so the air seemed to vibrate with the noise.

"The tank will overflow if this goes on," said Mum, shoving the plates into the dishwasher. "Mark, turn the radio off, would you? I don't want to listen to the news this morning. It's too depressing. Have you got your homework?"

"Yep."

"Are you sure?"

"Yep. Come on, Mum. I'll be late for the bus."

His mother looked up from the dishwasher, surprised. "We've got time."

"But it'll be slower because it's muddy. That's what you said yesterday."

"Maybe you're right. You run down the path first and I'll follow you, alright?"

The car was cold and smelled of wet dog.

"I shouldn't have let Bubbles ride in the car yesterday," said Mum, turning the window defroster to maximum. "Oh yuck, the smell's even worse with the heater on."

The car squelched through the puddles on the driveway, then squished onto the mud of the road.

"Mum?"

"Mmm?" Mum was concentrating on steering around the puddles. "Heaven knows when the county will get around to grading this road again."

"What's the longest time it's ever rained?"

"Good grief, I don't know. Forty days and forty nights. That's what it was supposed to be for Noah's flood. Oh, and for six weeks back in forty-seven, so your nanna told me. Fog and rain for six weeks."

"Six sevens are forty-two . . . that's forty-two days and beats Noah," said Mark with satisfaction. "Did it flood?"

"Right up to the garden fence where the veggie garden is now," said Mum. "Your nanna said no one could get out for weeks, and Mrs. Hilson down in the valley had her baby and they had to call a helicopter in . . . Oops, sorry about that," as the car plunged into a puddle. "I didn't realize it was so deep. Oh, look at that cow . . . get off the road, you stupid creature."

"Hey, Mum." Mark watched the cow slowly amble to the side of the road. "What do you know about Hitler?"

Mum blinked, and the car shot into another puddle. "Blast . . . Hitler? What brought that up?"

"Nothing," said Mark.

Mum shrugged. "You choose the worst times to ask questions. What do you want to know about him?"

"What was he like?"

"Oh, Mark, not now . . . it's bad enough trying to keep the car on the road with all this mud."

"Please, Mum, I want to know."

"Well, he was a monster, of course," said Mum reluctantly, still battling with the steering wheel. "All the concentration camps . . . and he killed all those Jews . . . Six million, I think, that's why it's called the Holocaust."

"Six million people?"

"There were lots of others he killed, too. Gypsies and people in trade unions . . . there was a TV program on it last year. It's hard to watch that sort of thing. I don't know why they put them on TV . . . Oh, he killed people who were disabled in some way, too . . . I think there was something like eleven million people altogether."

"Eleven million?" Mark tried to work it out. "That's

more than half the population of Australia."

"They weren't just in Germany," said Mum. "There were also camps in all the other countries he conquered. It was a long time ago, Mark."

The car bounced through another puddle. "Blast," said Mum again. "That nearly hit the muffler . . ."

"But why?" demanded Mark.

"What do you mean why?"

"Why did he do it?"

Mum shrugged. "That was the sort of person he was."

"But he must have had a reason!"

"I think he wanted to breed a Super Race," said Mum, trying to concentrate as she negotiated the puddles. "You know—Aryans. A pure Aryan race. So he had to get rid of anyone who didn't fit his idea, anyone who was different . . . Oh, look out you silly roo . . ."

The kangaroo watched them uneasily from the middle of the road, then jumped once, twice, and over the fence.

"I always wanted to be able to jump like that," said Mum, sighing in relief as the car hit the main road. "Oh, that reminds me—Jesse Owens. Yes, that was his name. He was a runner . . . I *think* he was a runner in the 1936

Olympics. Was he American? I can't remember. Your dad would know . . . Anyway, at that time the Olympics were in Germany and Hitler wanted to show the world what his Super Race could do, but then Jesse Owens won a whole lot of medals instead."

"What was so bad about that?" asked Mark.

"He was black!" exclaimed Mum. "And he beat all the Aryans hands down." The car drew to a stop slowly by the bus stop. "Hitler wouldn't even shake Jesse Owens' hand."

"How could someone as dumb as that run a country?" asked Mark.

"I don't know," said Mum. She glanced at her watch. "It's still pretty early."

"I don't mind," said Mark. He kissed her hurriedly. "See you."

"See you tonight. Don't worry if I'm a bit late. I need to get the books done before the inventory," said Mum. "Have a good day. Don't get too wet. Are you sure you've got your homework? How about your lunch money?"

"Yep, I'm sure. 'Bye Mum." The car trundled slowly back down the muddy road.

It must be Tracey's mum's turn to pick up Anna today. Mark hoped they'd be early too . . . Yes, there was the green truck, pulling out of Anna's driveway down the road.

Mark watched as Little Tracey hugged her mum and dashed for the bus shelter. Anna followed more slowly, the hood of her jacket shading her face.

"We got here early so Anna can go on with the story," announced Tracey. "She said she would. Didn't you, Anna?"

Anna nodded. "If you want," she said offhandedly.

"Yeah," said Mark, trying not to sound too enthusiastic. After all, it was just a story. Anna told lots of stories. "Better get a move on before Ben gets here and wants to put the Red Baron in it or something."

"Ben's not coming today. He's got a cold. His mum called my mum so I could tell Mrs. Latter not to wait for him." Anna pushed her wet hair back out of her eyes.

"Go on then!" urged Little Tracey impatiently.

"I'm not sure where to start," admitted Anna.

Mark was surprised. Anna always knew where to start. She'd never been stumped with a story before.

"What did Heidi have for breakfast?" demanded Little Tracey. "Did she have any pets? A dog? Or a horse?"

Anna relaxed. "I can tell you that," she said. "She had bread for breakfast—hot rolls coiled up into shapes with seeds on them. Sometimes they were caraway seeds and sometimes they were poppy seeds and once, for her birthday, the cook made her a bread roll in the shape of a cat, with a tail and poppy-seed eyes and whiskers.

"Like this." Anna traced a rough picture of a cat in the mud with the toe of her shoe. "And she liked it so much that her father ordered the cook to make her a bread cat every Monday, or a frog or a goat or a donkey. And once, for Easter, she made a sheep, too, with a whole lot of little baby lambs."

"Did Heidi eat them?"

Anna nodded. "She could eat them because every Monday morning there'd be another one. And she had milk for breakfast too, with some sugar in it."

"Then what did she do?" asked Little Tracey. "Did she go to school?"

Mark leaned back against the wall of the bus shelter. Anna's face had become animated, as it always was when she told a story, her hands flying and gesturing as though they wanted to tell the story too.

"No, she didn't go to school."

"Why not?" asked Mark, suddenly interested.

"Because . . ." Anna hesitated. "Because people might discover Hitler had a daughter. Or they might tease her about the mark on her face or maybe . . . maybe Hitler himself had hated school so he said his daughter didn't have to go. She had lessons with Fräulein Gelber instead."

"Didn't she go anywhere?" asked Little Tracey, disappointed.

"She went to church, I think," said Anna hesitantly. "I don't think she went every Sunday. Maybe it was only once or twice . . . I don't know." She shook her head. "It's just not working."

"How about start with, 'As far back as she could remember,'" Mark suggested. "Mr. McDonald got us to start an essay with that last term. You know: 'As far back as I can remember . . .'"

Anna took a deep breath. Her fingers looked white and cold and she shoved them in her pockets.

"As far back as Heidi could remember . . ." she began.

FOUR

As far back as Heidi could remember there had been Fräulein Gelber. Fräulein Gelber looked after her. She was tall and thin, with hips that looked like she had a coat-hanger in her skirt, and she had dark hair pulled back, and she wore narrow skirts that meant she couldn't run or walk too fast.

There also was Frau Mundt, who was a widow, and whose hands smelled of butter. Frau Mundt looked after her sometimes, when Fräulein Gelber visited her family.

Frau Mundt wore flowered skirts under her apron. Once she took Heidi on her knee and told her a story.

"We had no money, no work, no bread," she said. "Even if you had money, it was worth nothing in those days! A wheelbarrow full of money wouldn't buy you a loaf of bread.

"We begged. It was horrible, but we had to beg just to get food to eat. The occupying troops, the French and the Belgians, took all we had. They had whips and they whipped us off the sidewalks so we had to walk in the gutter. They threw us in the mud. That is how it was then, after the Great War.

"Then it was 1932. My Willi had a motorbike. It was an old motorbike, from before the war, but sometimes we got a little gas, and I sat on the backseat and we went to hear the Führer give a great speech. He wasn't the Führer then but it was so wonderful—thousands of people, oh, so many people cheering.

"And he told us how he wanted to be on the side of the unemployed—that was people like us, like me and Willi. He would save us, he would get us jobs, he would make Germany proud and free again, and I was cheering with everyone else while the tears ran down my cheeks.

"And that night I prayed that this great, good man would get all the votes so we could get out of need. He was the only one who gave us hope. And everything that he promised, he has given us."

It was only then that Heidi realized Frau Mundt was talking about Duffi.

Duffi was the Führer. He was her father too.

No one said he was her father, of course. She never called him Father. He hugged her whenever he visited, which wasn't often, and he brought her dolls with long blonde hair that made her cry secretly at night, because they were beautiful and she was not.

If she looked like the dolls he would have let her call him Father.

"But ... but how did she know she was his daughter if he never said?" objected Mark. "Sorry. I didn't mean to interrupt ..."

Anna shook her head. "I don't know," she said. "She just did. She lived there in his house—or the house he visited sometimes, anyway, when he wasn't in Berlin— and he called her 'my little girl.' 'How is my little girl today? Has she been good for Fräulein Gelber?'"

In the mornings she did her lessons with Fräulein Gelber and in the afternoons they walked.

Fräulein Gelber knew the name of every tree and every flower, and even the names of the grasses too.

"That's a cuckoo's call!" cried Fräulein Gelber, or, "Listen, there's a thrush."

Sometimes they took bread down to the carp in the pool by the bridge. One of the carp was big and black and gold. Fräulein Gelber said he was maybe two hundred years old as they threw the bread into the water for the fish.

When Heidi found hedgehogs freezing that winter Fräulein Gelber let her keep them in a basket by the hearth of the stove and Heidi fed them bread and milk.

"They will probably die anyway," said Fräulein Gelber indulgently, but she let her look after them. The hedgehogs didn't die, and in the spring Heidi let them go in the garden. She hoped that maybe they'd remember her and come back to her sometimes. It would be good to have friends, even if they were hedgehogs. But the hedgehogs scuttled away and Heidi didn't see them again.

Heidi always wanted to walk faster than Fräulein Gelber did. Fräulein Gelber didn't even have a limp, but she never walked quite fast enough.

There were so many things that Heidi would have liked to do. She would have liked to join the Bund Deutsche Mädel, the girl's association, like Frau Mundt's eldest daughter, Lotte. Frau Mundt told her lots of stories about Lotte. Heidi would have liked to meet her, but of course she never could. Heidi never met anyone at all.

If she joined the BDM she would do sports (Heidi had to ask Frau Mundt what sports were, but they sounded fun) and folk dancing. They would all sing songs together and, sometimes, go to the movies together.

But Heidi was not allowed.

She would have liked to go to school, to play with other girls. But that was not permitted either.

But she was a lucky girl. Everybody told her she was lucky. She had such pretty things—all the pretty things a girl could want.

She had her lovely home and such good food and Fräulein Gelber to look after her, and she had Duffi, who loved her, just as he loved all his German children.

Heidi hoped that one day Duffi would tell her that of all his German children he loved her best.

An engine sounded in the distance. A rumble coming closer, closer. Surely it was too early for the bus.

It was only Johnny Talbot on his motorbike, roaring up to town. He raised his hand briefly at the kids as he passed the shelter.

Anna sat still with her hands in her pockets.

"What . . .?" Mark broke off and tried to choose his words carefully. "How could she want someone like that to love her? Someone who did such horrible things."

"He was her father," said Anna simply.

"But what about the concentration camps? What about all the Jews he killed and the war?"

"She didn't know," said Anna.

"But she must have!"

Anna shook her head. "The concentration camps were secret. I mean, what they did there was secret. They were just supposed to be work camps. That's what it said in the papers. And Heidi didn't even see the papers. No one showed them to her. Only sometimes, when Duffi made a speech, Fräulein Gelber would cut out his photo for her to pin on the wall.

"How would she know what was happening? She didn't even go to school so she couldn't listen to other people talk."

"But she was there—in Hitler's house—in the middle of everything," objected Mark.

Anna nodded slowly. "She was in the middle of everything, but she knew less than anyone outside."

Anna put her hands in her lap, and her face got its storytelling look again. "She knew there was war. People talked about the war. But no one said that it was Hitler's fault. The people in the household worked for Hitler. They thought that he was wonderful and that's what they told Heidi.

"Hitler was the leader who was going to save Germany, who would bring about the Third Reich. Germany would reign over the world and all the shame of World War One would be wiped out. Why would Heidi think any differently?"

Mark shook his head. "But . . . but she must just have *known*. If she'd just started to think about it all . . ."

"Would you know if your parents were doing something wrong?" asked Anna softly.

"Of course I would. But they wouldn't do anything really wrong anyway."

"Are you sure?" persisted Anna. Her eyes were bright. "All the things your mum and dad believe in— have you ever really wondered if they are right or wrong? Or do you just think they're right because that's what your mum and dad think, so it *has* to be right?"

"Well, I . . ." Mark stopped.

No, he'd never thought Mum and Dad could be wrong, really wrong, about something. Something big— not just like Mum always wanting to be early and Dad cheering for Carlton even though he could see that they were losers (that's what Mum said at any rate).

But that was different. Mum and Dad weren't evil.

"It's not the same," he said at last.

Anna shrugged.

Little Tracey drummed her feet impatiently, "Go on with the story," she insisted. "*Please*, Anna."

Anna glanced at Mark. "Okay," she said.

"Sometimes, just sometimes, Heidi felt that maybe . . . maybe things weren't always . . . right."

It was the day after her birthday party. Duffi couldn't be there—Duffi came so rarely nowadays. He had all of Germany to look after, and the war. But she had had a cake, in spite of the war, though she'd heard one of the guards mutter how much butter it took to make it.

It seemed other people didn't have butter or cakes like that anymore.

"So there were guards?" asked Mark.

"Yes," said Anna. "There were always guards."

Duffi sent a doll from Paris. It had dark hair like her own, so Heidi liked it better than her other dolls, but it still didn't have a mark on its face and anyway she was much too old for dolls.

She sat the doll on the shelf above her bed with all the others and went to find Fräulein Gelber. It was time for Heidi's lessons. Fräulein Gelber had never been late before.

Fräulein Gelber was in the garden, sitting on the wrought-iron seat under the plum tree. She had a letter in her hand. She was crying. Her face was all scrunched up like a mouse's.

Heidi approached timidly. She didn't know what to do when someone cried.

"Fräulein Gelber?" she asked at last. "What's the matter?"

Fräulein Gelber thrust her handkerchief back into her pocket and tried to make her face look normal. "It's my brother," she said. "They're sending him to the Russian front. Oh, Heidi, it is insane, insane. He will die there, I know he will. We can never win this war now."

Then suddenly she looked frightened, her eyes red in her swollen face. She looked up at Heidi as though she had remembered who she was. She tried to smile.

"I'm being so silly," she said. "Please forget I said that, Heidi. Please forget I said anything at all. I am just worried for my brother—who would not be? But of course he will come back safely. Of course Germany will win the war."

Fräulein Gelber fumbled the letter into the pocket of

her jacket. "It's time for lessons," she said. "You are a very lucky girl, you know that? All these wonderful things that you're learning."

"Yes," said Heidi. "I know that I'm lucky."

Anna stopped.

"Go on," said Mark after a while.

"There was another time, another time that Heidi realized something was wrong."

It was one of the women in the kitchen who came to do the scrubbing.

She was crying, and the others were all comforting her.

"I didn't know," she kept saying. "I didn't know. They took her away. They said it was for the best, she would be cared for."

Frau Mundt saw Heidi listening and ran across the kitchen to her, and took her hand. "Freya isn't well. Come on, I'll take you upstairs."

Frau Mundt led her up the stairs, away from the sobbing below.

"Frau Mundt, what's wrong with her?"

Frau Mundt hesitated. "She has just found out that her sister is dead."

"When did she die? In the air raids?" Even Heidi knew about the air raids. The women in the kitchen were always talking about people they knew who had been killed or had their homes bombed in the raids.

"Not in the air raids. She has been dead, oh, six months maybe."

"I didn't know she had a sister," said Heidi.

"Her sister, she was not quite right in the head you understand, not clever like other children. So they took her to a special school. And now Freya has found out her sister is dead. No one told them she had died, not till the family wrote to say that they would visit next month. And now she thinks they killed her sister there."

"Did they kill her?" whispered Heidi.

"No, of course not. Of course they didn't," said Frau Mundt, just a bit too firmly. "Freya has just been listening to stories—silly stories, you know how people talk. But sometimes things like that have to happen. It's for the good of everyone. We cannot have weaklings in the new German race. People like Freya's sister mustn't be allowed to have children. It is like with the Jews."

"What are Jews?" asked Heidi. The word was familiar—she'd heard it before. She'd even read it in Duffi's book, the big, boring one that Fräulein Gelber kept on the mantelpiece and made her read a page from each day.

The book talked about the "Jewish problem" but Heidi had never known quite what it meant.

Frau Mundt bit her lip. "You should ask Fräulein Gelber about that. But it is all nonsense what they say. Nonsense. The Jews are simply being sent to work, that's all. The Jews are rich, everyone knows that. It's time they were made to work. Come on now, hurry upstairs."

Later, during their walk, she asked Fräulein Gelber, "Fräulein Gelber, who are the Jews?"

Fräulein Gelber scarcely hesitated in her stride. "The Jews are different. They are different from us. That is why the Führer wants to separate them. So they can't endanger the lifeblood of the German people, so they can't weaken it."

"What happens to them?"

"They are sent to camps. Places to work." She looked at her sharply. "Who has been telling you about the Jews?"

"No one. Well, Frau Mundt. But she said I was to ask you."

"Well, I've told you. They are different from us. That's why they have to be sent away."

"Are there any Jews near here?"

"No, of course not. But if one did escape and come near here, the guards would catch them and send them back. There is no need to worry."

"I'm not worried," said Heidi.

Anna's voice stopped.

"But what happened then?" demanded Mark. "Go on!"

Little Tracey nudged him. "The bus," she said. "Come on. The bus's here."

FIVE

IT WAS ONLY a story, Mark told himself that night after dinner. Just a story, nothing more. It wasn't true—but there were true things in it.

Maybe that's what puzzled him, Mark decided. None of Anna's other stories had had true things in them before.

The creek bubbled and twisted, brown and muddy in the growing dark just like the thoughts inside him. Mark could see it from the living room window and from his bedroom. You could even smell it from the house: year-old wombat droppings and cow manure, and rotten leaves and bark, all brewed up together like that herbal tea stuff Mum sometimes drank and Dad would never touch.

When he was younger, Mark used to watch the floods and wonder what it would be like to float down them on a raft. He'd float right out to sea perhaps and then along the coast, or maybe out to an island with palm trees and white sand.

But of course any raft would be torn to bits in the flood. You'd be drowned in a whirlpool or snagged by a log. It was fun to pretend though. Sometimes pretending could feel real.

And some of Anna's story *was* real. The bits about Hitler and the Jews.

"Dad?"

"Mmm?" Dad didn't look up from the pamphlet he was reading. "Mark, if it's trigonometry, ask your mum. You know what I'm like at math."

"No, it's not homework. I was just wondering. . . ."

"Wondering what?"

"Why did Hitler hate the Jews so much?" asked Mark in a rush.

Dad blinked and put the pamphlet down. "What brought this on?"

"Oh, just something at school," said Mark. Which was true in a way, he reflected.

"No idea," said Dad, glancing down at his pamphlet again, then looking dutifully back up at Mark. "How about asking Mrs. Holster at school?"

Mrs. Holster was the school librarian.

"Okay," said Mark, disappointed.

Dad looked at him a bit helplessly. "It wasn't just the Jews he killed," he said. "It was anyone who disagreed with him too. That all you wanted to know?"

Mark shook his head, thinking. "Dad?"

"Yes?" asked Dad, a bit warily.

"If you were Hitler . . ."

"If I was *who*?" Dad began to laugh.

"No, Dad, I'm serious. If you did things like Hitler did—really bad things—what do you think I should do?"

Dad looked at him more sharply. "You mean, should you go along with me because I'm your father, no matter what?"

"Yeah, that's about it," said Mark.

"I don't know," said Dad slowly. He put his paper down, as though for once he was seriously trying to answer Mark's question. "I suppose I'd want you to do what you thought was right.

"But . . ." Dad hesitated, then went on. "If we do ever disagree about things, I hope we'll still be able to talk about it. Still meet and be a family, no matter how much we argue."

"Okay," said Mark.

"Does that answer your question?"

"I don't know," said Mark truthfully. "Hey, what would you do if I was a mass murderer? You know, chopped people up with a chainsaw or something."

"Stop your allowance," said Dad, grinning. "And I'll tell you straight, kid—you murder one more person and there'll be no television for a month. And if you try burying the bodies under your mum's roses, I'll send you to your room. And you'd better clean the blood off my good chainsaw too."

"No—really."

"Dunno," said Dad, serious again. "Try to work out why you did it. Be sad for you. Be sad for your victims. Try to get help for you. Wonder how your mother and I failed you . . ."

"Would you turn me into the police?"

"Yes," said Dad slowly. "I suppose I'd have to. That's a hell of a question, Mark."

"Would you still love me? No matter what I did? Even if I killed hundreds and hundreds of people?"

"Yes, of course we would, you dingbat . . . or maybe we'd love you in a different way. What's brought all this on anyway?"

"Oh, nothing," said Mark.

41

SIX

THE RAIN CHATTERED onto the ground, and dribbled along the wet barbed wire around Harrison's paddock till it trickled down in short ploppy streams. It seemed even louder in the bus shelter.

The cows chomped sadly at the wet grass. Today the air was still, so the rain fell straight and clear. Mark, Anna, and Little Tracey had all arrived early once again.

"It's never going to stop," said Mark. "It's going to go on and on and we'll have to take a boat to school and all the cars will float away . . ."

"Really?" asked Little Tracey, wide eyed.

"No, of course not really," said Mark. "Hey Anna . . . I was wondering. Have you told anyone else this story? The Hitler one?"

"No," said Anna shortly. "It's just between us."

"Oh," said Mark, vaguely pleased.

"Are you going to tell us more?" Little Tracey

bounced up and down.

"If you like," said Anna.

It was soon after Heidi had asked Fräulein Gelber about the Jews that they had to move.

"Why do we have to go?" asked Heidi, half scared and half excited.

Fräulein Gelber waved a letter, typewritten, with a sprawling signature at the bottom, but too quickly for Heidi to read what it said.

"From Duffi?" asked Heidi.

Fräulein Gelber shrugged, as though to say that all orders came eventually from Duffi, but this letter was from someone else.

"Where will we go?" asked Heidi.

Fräulein Gelber told her. The name meant nothing to Heidi.

"We will look it up on the map this afternoon," said Fräulein Gelber. "It will be a nice place. You will like it."

"But *why* do we have to go?"

"It will be safer there," said Fräulein Gelber, but she didn't say for whom. She smiled. "It is much nearer my family," she added. "Only two, three hours away by bicycle."

"Will they visit us?" asked Heidi eagerly.

Sometimes Fräulein Gelber had let Heidi read her mother's letters or her sister's, or even her brother's, as a treat. Her father had died, many years before, and that was why Fräulein Gelber had to work. He had been a friend of Duffi's.

But Fräulein Gelber had told her often that it was an honor to work in the Führer's household. "I could have married," she had explained to Heidi. "I have had several offers. Several men have pleaded with me to marry them."

"Why didn't you?" asked Heidi, hoping that Fräulein Gelber would say, "I didn't want to leave you."

But instead she said, "To give up my work, after all the Führer has done for us? That I couldn't do."

"I don't think they will visit," said Fräulein Gelber now, in a voice that told Heidi not to ask why.

Suddenly a thought occurred to her. "Will Duffi be at the new house?"

Perhaps that was why they were going, so they could be with Duffi. Maybe Duffi missed her. Maybe he had said . . .

"No, of course not," said Fräulein Gelber. "He is in Berlin."

"But will he visit?"

"Perhaps," said Fräulein Gelber.

Other people packed for them. Heidi only had to pack her dolls and her special books.

Half of her wanted to leave the dolls behind—the pretty, perfect dolls—but Duffi had given them to her and, besides, she'd have had to explain to Fräulein Gelber.

They traveled to the new house by car the next day. Their move must have been arranged even before Fräulein Gelber had been told.

Three soldiers came to help them.

One of the soldiers drove their car, another rode behind on a motorbike, and the other drove the car with their luggage.

It was only an hour's journey, but it was the first time Heidi had ever been in a car. (No, there had been one time before, when Duffi had taken her for a drive. He had pointed out a lake and geese and made her laugh by making goose noises, but that was so very long ago it was hard to remember.)

She had never been so far before. There was so much that was new to see: the fields that were much like the fields she knew, but yet different, and pale brown cows, and once, a pair of goats in an orchard. The goats had climbed up onto a table and were stretching up to eat the trees, and Heidi laughed and pointed them out to Fräulein Gelber.

She would have liked to ask the soldier to stop the car so she could watch the goats, but she had been told already that she was not to talk to him.

No one said why she had to be silent, but she guessed. The driver was not to know who she was.

Suddenly there was a humming, far up in the sky, like bees in the plum blossoms, but too sharp to be bees. The humming deepened, closer and closer, and then engines could be heard.

The driver glanced at Fräulein Gelber, then pulled the car in under a tree, so they couldn't be seen from the air. The car behind pulled in close to the hedge, and so did the motorbike driver.

"Bomber," said the driver briefly.

The enemy plane seemed to come slowly, slowly, slowly; then suddenly the plane was almost above them, and coming fast.

"Perhaps we should get out and lie on the ground, just in case they see the car," said Fräulein Gelber nervously.

"Too late," said the driver. "They'd see us move."

Heidi craned to get a better look out the window.

Would they hear the sound of a bomb falling before it hit their car and killed them, Heidi wondered in sudden terror.

Fräulein Gelber pulled her back, as though just seeing the plane might make her more vulnerable, but Heidi caught a glimpse of it anyway, and saw its black shadow flying across the grass beyond the trees.

How could death come so quickly over the trees, wondered Heidi. She watched the shadow till it was out of sight, and the engine noise had faded to humming again.

Fräulein Gelber took her hand. Fräulein Gelber's hand was damp and clammy, and shaking too. The driver started the car, and they drove off again.

More trees and fields, and once, a village, with a church at one end of the square and a cafe at the other, with no bomb damage at all that Heidi could see, except for one house on the outskirts, half ruined, and the windows filled up with cardboard instead of glass.

"Stray bomb, probably," said the driver, nodding at it. "Sometimes they have a few spare that they haven't dropped on targets and they drop them anywhere, so that they don't use up so much fuel carrying them back home."

Home was England. England was the enemy. Sometimes Heidi wondered what it must be like to be English. Were they evil people or just stupid? How could they possibly win against all of Germany, against Duffi. England was such a little island on the map.

The road twisted out of the village, past a farm, and then another, with pigs rolling in the fresh black mud, and then down another road, past two ancient oak trees like giant dark umbrellas across the road, and then they were there.

The new house was small, or at least it seemed so to Heidi after the big house where she'd lived before. It crouched under the trees like it, too, was hiding from the bombs.

But it had three bedrooms up narrow twisting wooden stairs: one bedroom was for Heidi and one was for Fräulein Gelber. The third was to be their school-room, where all their books would go. It had a big kitchen with a cold, paved floor and an even bigger cellar that you got to by going out the kitchen door and down some steps.

Fräulein Gelber inspected the cellar thoroughly. She didn't say why, but Heidi knew that the cellar was where they would go if enemy planes flew overhead.

Bombs might crush the house, but the cellar would be safe.

The cellar smelled sweet and musty. It had bins of apples stored in old dried leaves, and shelves with jars of jam and sauerkraut and honey, and cabbages all in a pile and two sacks of potatoes with just a few taken out of one, and a sack of golden onions, their skins floating off like yellow autumn leaves.

"Where are the people who lived here before?" asked Heidi, but Fräulein Gelber couldn't say.

"That's none of our business," she said, though Heidi thought it was. It seemed odd to be wandering through rooms that other people had lived in not long ago eating their onions and plum jam, and then not even to know what they'd been like or where they were now.

Only Heidi and Fräulein Gelber were to live in the house. Sergeant Amchell lived in the barn.

He was old, with a long salt-and-pepper moustache that looked like it would fall out if he blew his nose too hard. He had been wounded in the leg in the last war, so he limped just like Heidi.

She hoped he'd notice that she limped too, and maybe joke about it—the two of them with only two good legs between them—or something friendly like that, but he kept to himself and tended the giant cabbages in the garden instead of standing at attention at the door like the other guards she'd known. Mostly he pretended he didn't see her when she smiled at him, or hear her when she said "Good morning."

He was the only guard they had now.

The first night in the new house Fräulein Gelber lit candles and sat her on one of the hard dark chairs in the sitting room.

"A farm woman will be coming tomorrow to cook the food, and to look after the house," said Fräulein Gelber. "Her name is Frau Leib. She has been told you are my niece, the child of my sister who was killed in the air raids."

Heidi looked up. "Was your sister killed in the air raids?" she asked in alarm.

Fräulein Gelber's sister was married and lived three streets away from her mother. She had sent Fräulein Gelber a scarf last Christmas. Heidi had secretly hoped that one day someone from Fräulein Gelber's family might send her a present too, but they never did. Perhaps Fräulein Gelber had never mentioned Heidi in her letters. Or maybe they thought she had everything she needed and didn't need presents.

"No, of course not," said Fräulein Gelber. "My sister is quite well, aside from a slight case of influenza last month. But it's best if that's what Frau Leib continues to believe."

Fräulein Gelber hesitated. "I don't want you speaking too much to her, you understand?"

"I understand," said Heidi.

SEVEN

Frau Leib had gray hair, not speckled gray like Fräulein Gelber's—whose hair looked a bit like a hen's feathers, Heidi thought sometimes—but gray all over like a saucepan, and tight curls that looked like they were made of metal too, they were so firm about her head.

Frau Leib's hands were large, with red knuckles. Her skirt was much longer and wider than Fräulein Gelber's, the sort of skirt you could use for carrying apples or cabbages from the cellar, and an apron from her neck to her knee that seemed welded to her waist no matter what else she wore.

Heidi never saw Frau Leib without her apron; whether she was coming or going, she still had it on. It looked bigger than she was, all bunched up at her sides, as though at one time Frau Leib had been even larger than she was now.

Frau Leib lived on the farm just down the road, the

one with the pigs in the black mud. Her husband worked the fields with their young grandsons and two of their daughters-in-law. Their sons were away fighting, except for one who was in a prisoner-of-war camp in America (America was the enemy now too).

Herr Leib was in the Nazi Party—one of the first members in the whole district—so his wife was trust-worthy.

She also liked to talk.

Frau Leib talked in a dialect so thick it was sometimes hard to understand, but that didn't matter, because she said so much that you could leave half of it out and still have enough for conversation.

"I talk as the pig's snout grows," said Frau Leib with a grin that showed the dark gaps in her back teeth, meaning that she talked as thoughts flew into her head, and there were a lot of thoughts under Frau Leib's gray curls.

"What happened to your face, girl?" she demanded, as soon as she saw Heidi. "A burn? Is that what it is? The bombs?"

"I was born with it," said Heidi quietly.

Frau Leib's great arms came round her and she hugged her to her apron, which had just the faintest smell of pig. "You poor darling," she said. "I will give you some ointment. It's pig lard, with chickweed and other herbs. It is my grandmother's recipe and she got it from her mother, so it is very good. It takes scars like that away so fast you'd think the boar was after them to get its fat back!"

"Thank you," said Heidi, as she was released from the apron, though she knew the ointment wouldn't do any good. If there had been a way to remove the mark Duffi would have arranged it years before.

But there were some questions even Frau Leib knew not to ask. Whoever had organized the house for them had made it clear that Fräulein Gelber—and Heidi—were people of importance. Their clothes, their food, their lack of ration cards, the guard, the provisions that arrived for them every second Monday were proof enough of that.

But even if Frau Leib didn't ask questions, she still liked to talk.

"Listen to the frogs in the pond!" said Frau Leib, her fat fingers firm around the knife handle as she chopped through thick bacon while Heidi peeled the potatoes for the soup. (Heidi had never had bacon before—Duffi didn't like people to eat meat. But they ate it now.) "If the frogs croak like that at night it will rain in the morning."

"Are there fish in the pond?" asked Heidi. She was allowed in the kitchen often now to help Frau Leib. Together they made the beds, and dusted too.

"Just the frogs," said Frau Leib.

Frau Leib had five children: Lisl and Franz and Josef and Helmuth and Erna.

She also had two grandsons who worked the farm, and another two who were only babies, too young to help at all.

"But oh, we need the help," said Frau Leib, shaking her head so her chins wobbled but her metal curls stayed firm. "All the fine strong men are in the army, and just old men and boys to help us now."

If the farm had been bigger, she explained, the boys—her sons—might have been given a deferment from the army, so they could help the Führer by growing food for the soldiers of the Reich.

"Of course, they are proud to be fighting too," said Frau Leib hurriedly, with a sideways look at Heidi. "We all have to do what we can."

Several times Heidi noticed Frau Leib slip a little flour or a twist of sugar into the pocket of her coat that was hung by the back door when she came to work. But Heidi did not speak of it. She and Fräulein Gelber had more than they needed, and she now knew from Frau Leib that most people were going hungry, even here in the country with the cows and goats and pigs.

Frau Leib took their scraps to feed to the hens, and the dishwater to feed to the pigs. "It will just go to waste anyhow," said Frau Leib reasonably, as she slipped a piece of leftover sausage into the hens' bin that they could very well have had for lunch the next day.

"Could we keep hens?" Heidi asked Fräulein Gelber.

Fräulein Gelber shook her head. "They are dirty things," she said. "Besides, Frau Leib will sell us all the eggs we need."

It was odd with Frau Leib in the kitchen. No one had ever talked to Heidi so freely before. Sometimes Heidi thought that Frau Leib wasn't talking to her, but was just talking because she was uncomfortable when her mouth was still.

But it was good to listen to Frau Leib's conversation. There was so much to learn that no one had ever mentioned to her before.

". . . and the blacksmith keeps the cows shod—oh yes, the cows must have shoes just like the horses if they are to work—and the scythes whetted . . . You have never seen the blacksmith work? But all the children hang

56

around the forge after school! The banging and the clanging and the hot fire . . . you must come down this afternoon then . . . but perhaps not," said Frau Leib, pushing the broom and remembering.

"It's the fat that makes a good pig," explained Frau Leib one day, as she worked the pastry on the thick marble board. "The fat not only gives flavor, you understand, it helps the meat keep well. A sausage without fat is tasteless, but it also dries out, and sometimes goes bad. But not all food will put fat on a pig of course. Fat produces fat—that's what you have to remember. Corn is good, because corn is yellow like fat is yellow."

"I have brought you a present," Frau Leib said one day, as she took off her hat and gloves and coat and hung them on the peg by the door.

"What is it?" asked Heidi.

Frau Leib smiled. "It's in my coat pocket."

Heidi peered into the pocket. There was something in the bottom; something small and warm.

"A rabbit!" she cried, lifting it out. The rabbit was soft and black and white and it twitched its nose.

"It's a doe," said Frau Leib, smiling. "When she gets bigger you can breed it to our buck and then you'll have lots of rabbits, and I'll show you how to make rabbit pie."

"Look at its whiskers!" cried Heidi, delighted. "Thank you, Frau Leib!"

"You're a good girl," said Frau Leib, and Heidi knew it wasn't because she was polite, or helped make the beds, but because she had said nothing about the things in Frau Leib's pockets.

Heidi helped Frau Leib in the mornings, and often in the afternoons now as well. Fräulein Gelber had arranged all the schoolbooks in the third bedroom, but she no longer seemed as interested in lessons as she was before.

She didn't even make Heidi read pages from Duffi's book. She read her letters from home over and over, and several times Heidi found her crying. But now she wouldn't explain why.

Fräulein Gelber still liked to walk, and they did walk once a day, but not along the lane: "In case someone sees us and asks questions," said Fräulein Gelber. They walked across the fields instead.

The fields had belonged to their house. Frau Leib's husband worked them now. They walked across the Leibs' fields too. There was a wood not far away and once they saw a deer, grazing delicately by the edge of the trees, and once a wild pig.

The wild pig did not look at all like Frau Leib's pigs. It was black and hairy with big shoulders and a tiny back and even its snout was crooked. It stared at them with tiny eyes, and then it ran away.

Heidi asked Fräulein Gelber why the wild pig was so different from Frau Leib's pigs, but Fräulein Gelber couldn't say. "It's just the way things are," she said.

There were wild mushrooms in the fields in autumn and the leaves in the wood fluttered like yellow butterflies and stuck to Heidi's shoes. Frau Leib made mushroom omelette as a treat, because even for them, eggs were getting scarce.

Sometimes city women came out and tried to trade things, like a cushion or a good saucepan, for an egg. Or even jewelry for a ham.

Frau Leib told Heidi all about the city women, but she didn't say whether she traded with them or not. It was illegal to trade food. Everything was rationed; but Heidi suspected that she did, even if Herr Leib didn't know.

One day when she and Fräulein Gelber were out in the fields, a plane flew down so low she could see the pilot's face, or rather, his helmet, which mostly hid his face. All she could really see were his mouth and chin, white below the brown helmet.

She almost wanted to wave, he was so close. If she'd yelled "Hello" he might even have heard her above the clatter of the engines. But he was an enemy, and even if he had been a German pilot, Fräulein Gelber would have frowned.

EIGHT

Mʀ. McDonald was sitting at his table marking homework when Mark looked through the door.

"Mark, what's up?" he asked.

"Nothing . . . I just wanted to ask you something."

"Sure. Fire away," he said.

"I just wanted to know . . ." began Mark slowly. "I mean it's silly but I was thinking. Do kids have to be like their parents?"

Mr. McDonald frowned. "I'm not sure I get your meaning," he said.

"Well, say someone's father did something really evil . . . like Hitler, or Pol Pot," he added hurriedly. "Would their kids be evil too?"

Mr. McDonald looked relieved, as though he'd expected the question to be more difficult.

"That's a good question, Mark. No, they probably wouldn't be evil too. I can't think of anyone really bad in history whose children were as bad as they were. In fact, sometimes the opposite was true. Bad people often have good kids, and good people have bad kids."

"But we're like our parents, aren't we?"

"Yes and no," said Mr. McDonald. "Kids often inherit the same sort of temperament as their parents, and maybe the same talents. Like music for instance, or painting. But usually they do something different with it. A painter's kid might become an architect, for example, if they inherited the same talent. Maybe that's the best way to put it—you inherit your talents from your parents, but what you do with them is your own choice. And mostly kids do things their parents never thought of."

"So . . . Pol Pot's kids for example. They wouldn't go around killing people?"

"I don't know if Pol Pot had any kids," said Mr. McDonald.

"But if he did?"

Mr. McDonald hesitated. "Well, if they were in the Khmer Rouge—Pol Pot's army—I suppose they might do the same sort of things. But if they were brought up somewhere else, then no, they probably wouldn't do the same sort of things at all." Mr. McDonald looked at him sharply. "Why do you ask, Mark?"

"I was just wondering," said Mark.

"There isn't any trouble at home is there?" asked Mr. McDonald carefully.

Suddenly Mark realized what he meant.

"No! I mean, no, I'm not worried about Dad or anyone." Mark nearly laughed. "I saw something on Pol Pot on TV that's all, and I wondered if he had a son and what he'd be like."

"Maybe he decided to be a chef, or a banker. But he'd probably feel guilty and confused if he realized what his father had done," said Mr. McDonald.

"It wouldn't be his fault, would it? All the murders his dad did?"

"No," said Mr. McDonald slowly. "It wouldn't be his fault at all. Not unless he felt the same way as his dad did. Or maybe if he refused to face up to the evil things his dad had done . . . that would be wrong. If we don't face up to things that were wrong in the past then we might do them again."

"Mr. McDonald . . ." Mark had another question, but he could see that Mr. McDonald was getting impatient.

"Yes, Mark?"

"The things Hitler did, or Pol Pot . . . I mean could they have ever thought they were right?"

Mr. McDonald looked uncomfortable. "I don't know," he said at last. "Sometimes people think they are doing the right thing even when it is bad. But with Hitler and Pol Pot . . . I just don't know. Maybe they did think what they were doing was good."

"But how can we *know* we're doing the right thing?" asked Mark.

Mr. McDonald shrugged. "I can't answer that either," he said a bit helplessly. "I'd have to think about it. How about you ask your parents . . . or Father Steven next Sunday . . . I'm sorry if that doesn't really answer your question. I had better go and grab some lunch before the bell rings. No more questions then?" he asked hopefully.

"No more questions. Thanks," said Mark.

He supposed Mr. McDonald had at least *tried* to give him answers.

The thought pestered him all afternoon at school.

People *should* do what they think is right. But what if what you think is right, is wrong?

Doing what everyone else did was no help either. If there was one thing that all that Hitler stuff showed, it was that most of a whole country could be wrong.

Had everyone back then *really* thought about things?

Had they looked at the evidence or did they just believe because they wanted to believe, because they wanted to?

There had to be some answer, thought Mark.

Someone must have an answer somewhere.

NINE

THE BUS TRUNDLED through town, dropping off a couple of kids on the outskirts, then taking the turnoff down to Wallaby Creek.

Mark watched the gray sky and the wet paddocks beyond. Feehan's Swamp was like a mirror, dull silver reflecting bare willows and cold cows. Even the road looked a deeper gray.

He was sick of the rain. It just sat there, as if it was too lazy to move. It wasn't even a proper rain any more—just wet air, cold and bleak and boring.

"Hey, did you work out the question on page seventy-six last night?" demanded Bonzo beside him.

"Sort of," said Mark.

"I asked Mum, but she wasn't any use at all. Didn't parents ever learn anything at school? They can't ever answer anything right."

"Yeah," said Mark.

Bonzo looked at him more closely.

"Hey, are you alright?"

"Sure." Mark sat up. Too much thinking, that's what was wrong, he thought to himself.

"What are you doing this weekend?" asked Bonzo.

Mark blinked. He'd forgotten it was Friday. That meant they couldn't play the Game tomorrow morning. No more story till Monday.

Bonzo nudged him.

"Dunno," said Mark. Maybe the three of them could meet on Saturday or something, he wondered. But of course everyone would think that was really odd. He and Anna hadn't spent any time together since they played together as little kids, and as for Little Tracey . . .

"We could go for a bike ride," said Bonzo. "Dad could put the bikes into the back of the truck when he goes up to town and we could ride back to my place."

Mark shrugged. "Sure. If the rain stops, anyway. Bonzo . . ." asked Mark suddenly.

"Mmmm?" Bonzo was still staring out at the rain.

"What would you do if someone wanted to start a . . . a sort of army around here?"

"You mean all us kids drilling with rifles and things to attack invaders? It'd be cool."

"But . . . but what if it wasn't invaders. I mean, say if it was a politician who started it all, like Hitler, and they wanted us to attack people they didn't like. . . ." Mark stopped. He didn't know how to explain.

"Like who? I still think it'd be cool," said Bonzo. "Maybe New Zealand would invade us . . . or UFOs . . . and we'd have to fight them and all dress up in uniforms and maybe ambush them like on that show on TV . . ."

"That wasn't what I meant," began Mark.

Anna would understand, he thought, his eyes on her in the seat in front. Anna really thought about things. All he had to do was nudge her, and say, "How about you and Little Tracey come down to my place tomorrow afternoon and you can finish the story . . ."

But it would be embarrassing. He knew he couldn't do it.

TEN

THE FLOOD SMELLED like wet socks.

Even the kitchen was full of the smell and it was stronger than the smell of last night's pizza.

Mark shut the kitchen door—Dad must have left it open when he went out to check that the pump was still out of reach of the flood—then sat down at the kitchen table. Behind him the radio sang out the tune that announced the news. Dad had listened to the weather report earlier and left the radio on:

"*. . . the genocide still continues. Eyewitnesses now say that the death toll may number several thousands, with the numbers still rising as government troops . . .*"

Mark blinked. For a moment he had thought he was back in the 1930s, the radio talking about all the people that Hitler was killing.

But this was *now*. People were being killed *now*. He'd heard these reports before of course, but it had never seemed real . . . he'd never actually *thought* about it before.

The radio announcer was talking about something different. Something about land rights and . . .

"Well, who's ready for breakfast?" demanded Dad happily, tramping into the kitchen in his socks and turning the radio off. "I'm starved!"

Dad always cooked eggs and bacon on Saturday mornings. Saturday was the only day he cooked breakfast, and the only day they had eggs and bacon, with a sausage each and baked beans sometimes as well. Fried cholesterol, Mum called it, but she liked Saturday breakfasts too.

Dad cracked the eggs into the pan with the sausages, leaving the eggshells on the counter. Then he took the bacon out of the microwave. He dumped the plates down on the table and sat down.

"Anyone want anything from town?" he asked, as he squirted chili sauce on his bacon. "I have to go up and get some more gas."

Mum shook her head. "I shopped last Thursday . . . well, maybe fresh bread. And milk. And shampoo, we've nearly run out . . . I'll make a list."

"Dad . . ." asked Mark suddenly.

"Mmm," said Dad, sprinkling pepper over his eggs.

"Are people being exterminated today?"

"Are they *what!*" Dad choked in surprise.

"Being exterminated. You know—like Hitler and the Jews."

Dad took a gulp of coffee. "Of course not," he said.

"But on the news it just said about people being killed in that place with the funny name . . ."

"I wasn't really listening," admitted Dad. "Look, don't worry your head about it, Mark. It's all a long way away."

Mark chewed for a minute. "Dad . . ." he asked.

"Now what?"

"How did great-great-grandpa get our farm?"

"What? He bought it." Dad reached for the mustard and squirted some on his sausage.

"He didn't steal it from the Aborigines?"

"No, of course not." Dad gave him a sharp look. "It wasn't like that in those days, anyway. No one thought of it as stealing."

"Mark, your eggs are getting cold," said Mum.

Mark took a bite of egg. "But what if he *did* take it from the Aboriginal people . . . just suppose. It wouldn't be our fault, would it?"

"Who's been feeding you all that stuff?" demanded Dad.

"I was just listening to the news, and someone said—"

"The things they teach kids nowadays," said Dad, attacking his sausage savagely. "It'd make more sense if they taught everyone to mind their own business."

"But Dad—"

"Mark, give it a rest would you?"

"But remember you told me that if we disagreed about anything we should talk about it. You said—"

"Mark, that's enough," said Mum sharply. "Okay?"

Mark ate his breakfast in silence.

The rain stopped on Saturday night. The clouds that had stretched tight and gray across the sky shrank into mushrooms that puffed and waddled through the blue. The trees shone tiny diamonds across their leaves and the creek shrank slightly under its edge of foam.

Sunday night the rain began again.

At least we had part of Sunday free, thought Mark gloomily, as he listened to the rain on the roof; the thud, thud, thud and the droop, droop, droop where it dripped from the eaves. Finally, he dozed.

He dreamed of the creek, and the flood smashing its

way across the rocks. He dreamed that Hitler was across the creek, but this Hitler wore jeans and his haircut was modern in spite of the moustache under his nose that looked as if it was sticky-taped on.

Hitler was making a speech. And suddenly there were people all around on Mark's side of the creek, listening, cheering.

"Go away," Mark yelled to them. "It's a silly speech! Can't you hear it's silly."

But his voice made no sound.

There was Ben on his motorbike with a swastika on his arm, and Bonzo in a uniform, and even Little Tracey was saluting Hitler too. Bonzo just wanted excitement and Ben didn't think about things at all and Little Tracey would do what her friends . . . "But he's wrong!" cried Mark. "Can't you see he's wrong!"

But they were laughing and cheering and excited, and no one was listening to Mark. They were wading into the creek, into the flood. They'd be washed away, thought Mark, and anyway, they shouldn't be there at all. It wasn't their farm and Dad would be angry with all the strangers on it . . . and the radio was talking about people being killed in Africa, in Europe, in Indonesia, and Hitler was laughing, laughing, laughing . . .

"You are all my children," screamed Hitler. "None of you question. You are all Hitler's children!"

"Go away," cried Mark again. "Can't you see I'm trying to sleep?"

And suddenly he must have woken, or half woken anyway, because he was in bed and the people were gone. He rolled over, and pulled the quilt up to his head, and this time he slept deeply.

The dream had almost vanished at breakfast. Only the flavor of it lingered inside his head.

"Mum?"

"Mmm? Do you want muesli or porridge this morning?"

"Porridge," said Mark. "Mum, if Hitler came back now . . ."

"You're not still going on about Hitler are you?" asked Mum, measuring the rolled oats into the bowl. She slipped it into the microwave and pressed the button. "You've got Hitler on the brain lately."

Mark watched the bowl spin around and around inside the microwave. "Well, not Hitler then. But someone really bad, like Hitler."

"Oh, Mark, not more questions. It's too early!" protested Mum.

"But Mum, what if *everyone* thought the really bad person was right! Like all the German people thought Hitler was right?"

Mum took the bowl from the microwave and stirred the porridge, then put it back again. "I don't think *all* the German people thought Hitler was right," she said. "Don't forget it was a totalitarian country."

"What's that mean?"

"It means Hitler controlled the radio and the newspapers, so no one was allowed to say anything he didn't agree with. And if you tried to speak out you were sent to a concentration camp."

"Did people protest?" asked Mark.

"No idea," said Mum. "I suppose so . . . Here you are." She passed him the milk and brown sugar.

"Mum, if Hitler had been in power . . . would you have protested?"

"Of course," said Mum.

"Even if it meant going to prison."

"What? No, I don't suppose so . . . Mark, I'm just not interested in stuff like that. Alright? Just eat your breakfast."

Mark sprinkled the sugar over his porridge. "What I mean is," he said, swallowing the first spoonful and blowing on the next. "If everyone—or almost every-one—thinks something is right, but you *know* it's wrong, what do you do then?"

"Mark, love, we don't have time for this! Just eat your porridge, okay? We'll be late."

Mark shrugged and took another spoonful of porridge. There was no point keeping on if Mum had had enough.

He wondered what it would be like to have a mum who *loved* answering questions. A mum who really liked thinking about things . . .

"That's a really good question, Mark," the imaginary Mum would say. "My first reaction is to say, 'Mind your own business.' But that's the wrong answer, isn't it?"

"Is it?" asked Mark in his mind.

The imaginary Mum would nod. "It's what I do all the time," she'd say slowly. "Turn off the TV, avoid arguments with people who want to discuss everything and sign petitions and things. But . . ." and she'd shake her head. "That's what people in Germany did, didn't they? They didn't agree with Hitler. Or not with everything he did. But they went along with it, till it was too late. They simply shut their eyes and let things happen." The imaginary Mum would nod her head and look at him seriously. "You've made me think a bit," she'd say.

And then she'd start listening to the news all the time and going to demonstrations and signing petitions.

And maybe Mum would have to go to prison if someone like Hitler did get into power, and there was no way he wanted her to go to prison.

But maybe . . . maybe . . .

"What's up?" asked Mum . . . the real Mum. "Porridge too hot?"

"It's okay," said Mark.

Mum sighed again. "Look, ask me questions when I'm not so rushed. Okay?"

"Okay," said Mark.

ELEVEN

THERE WAS STILL no sign of Ben at the bus stop on Monday.

"He must have a *really* bad cold," said Anna.

"His mum told my mum she didn't want him going to school in the rain in case it got worse," said Little Tracey. "'Cause he gets asthma sometimes when he gets a cold. Come on, Anna!"

"Come on what?" asked Anna.

"Go on with the story about Heidi," said Little Tracey.

For a moment Mark thought she was going to refuse—would say she'd forgotten how it went over the weekend or something like that.

But instead, Anna began, and the story flowed as if there had been no break, as though it was as clear as a movie in her mind, and all she was doing was describing what she saw and heard on the screen inside her mind.

"Frau Leib brought her news one morning," said Anna, her voice clear and low. "Along with the fresh goat's milk in the bright green china jug with the flowers on it."

Two of Frau Leib's nannies were ready for milking now. One was called Lottie and the other Hildegard, after two old friends of Frau Leib. Heidi wasn't at all certain if she would want a goat named after her but she never said so to Frau Leib, and sure enough, the next baby goat was called Heidi.

Frau Leib waited till Fräulein Gelber had gone upstairs to write the letters she seemed to be so often writing now.

Frau Leib seemed to know that Fräulein Gelber wouldn't approve of gossip, particularly the gossip she had today.

"They sent him away!" she whispered excitedly, as she stoked the fire in the old cracked stove. "Just last night, and Lisl came running over to tell me this morning."

"Your daughter? What did she say? Sent who away?" asked Heidi.

"Herr Henssel!" Her voice was happily horrified.

"He has the farm over past the mill. No one would have guessed! None of us guessed!"

"Guessed what?" wondered Heidi, but Frau Leib went on as though she hadn't heard.

"His sister married a draper in town." She lowered her voice and brought her wide, shiny face close to Heidi's. "A *Jewish* draper. The sister and her husband disappeared a long time ago, and everyone thought they had been taken to the camps. Herr Henssel never spoke of them. But Herr Henssel has been sheltering his sister and her husband all the time! He has been hiding them so they wouldn't take them to the work camps! Someone must have seen, someone must have noticed, and they must have notified the authorities, because today they took him away—took them *all* away. Oh, it is awful!" but Frau Leib's small eyes had the joyous gleam of a good gossip nonetheless.

"If the Jews just go to the camps to work, why did Herr Henssel have to hide them? Are the camps so terrible?" asked Heidi.

Frau Leib shrugged. She didn't care what the camps were like. The things that were important happened in her village, or to people she knew.

"Are there any other Jews near here?" asked Heidi.

"Not in our village, not any more. But before the war, in town, there were the Solomons, of course, in the drapers' shop—not that I ever went there, you understand. My husband would have been angry if I went to a Jewish shop. And there was Herr, oh, what was his name? The teacher at the school, and the doctor, not the new one, the old one. One of his children went to school with Gerta, who married my . . . but you know that, I showed you the photo of the wedding, and the Führer sent a copy of his book with his signature just inside the cover. Not that I have ever read it. I have sometimes taken it and looked inside. I have looked at it often. Such a wise clever book. But now, of course, all the Jews have been sent to the camps . . ."

"Heidi!" Fräulein Gelber stood at the door. "What are you doing?"

"Helping Frau Leib," said Heidi.

Fräulein Gelber fixed them both with one of her hardest looks. It was evident she had heard at least the last part of the conversation.

"It is time for your lessons," she announced, although the only lessons they had had recently were the passages Heidi read at night by the light of the candles on the table and the fire in the stove, while Fräulein Gelber sewed or looked at the flames as though she were far away and listening to a voice that was not Heidi's at all.

"Yes, Fräulein Gelber," said Heidi.

TWELVE

"**I**'VE GUESSED WHAT happens now," said Mark.

They were at the bus shelter. ("You want to go early *again?*" Mum had demanded in disbelief.)

The rain continued to melt from the clouds. Ben was still in bed with his cold.

"What?" asked Little Tracey eagerly.

"I bet Heidi organized some escape plan for the Jews from the concentration camp. Now she's found out what's happening, I mean. Or she spies on Hitler and passes on the information."

Anna looked at him steadily. "Would you spy on your father?" she asked him quietly.

"No," said Mark. "But my dad isn't Hitler."

Anna shook her head. "How could she spy on him? It had been months since she'd seen him. And even then just for a few minutes. Who would she pass information on to? Besides, she didn't know all that much—she didn't even know they were all meant to be killed in the camps. She only knew enough to wonder: what were Jews like? That's what no one seemed to be able to tell her. Just that they were different.

"Well, she was different too. And somehow she built up a picture of Jews in her mind. Jews were people just like her, with red marks on their faces and one leg just a little short. Different people, who had to be hidden away."

"So she did try to help them?" asked Mark at last.

Anna shrugged. "Sort of. She made a plan. She'd keep a watch out for any Jews who came to their garden, who needed help. And she'd hide them in the old hen-house down past the orchard where no one went except in summer when the plums were ripe."

It was easy at first. She told Fräulein Gelber that she was going to clean out the hen-house for the rabbits, for when the doe had babies.

Then she shoveled out the muck. It was the first time she had held a spade and her hands became sore. She spread fresh straw down. Fräulein Gelber gave Frau Leib money for the straw and Frau Leib's husband brought it to the house.

It didn't look too bad when she had finished.

There had to be food, too. That was the next part of the plan. When they came to the garden for shelter she would have to feed them. She could take a little from the kitchen of course, but it might not be enough.

So she took jars from the cellar, just one each day—things like plum jam and cherries in liqueur and honey—and she hid them in the hay. There were some tins in the kitchen and she'd have liked to take them too, but Fräulein Gelber might have noticed and blamed Frau Leib. If she and Frau Leib both took food from the kitchen, Fräulein Gelber was sure to notice sooner or later.

It took her a month, and then it was finished. Then she settled down to wait.

"When did the Jews come?" asked Little Tracey eagerly.

"They never came," said Anna. "Of course they never came. It was late in the war by then and they were in concentration camps and very few escaped from those. But it was all that she could do."

"But surely she could have done *something* else?" demanded Mark.

"What? Locked herself in her room and said she wasn't coming out or wouldn't eat till they shut down the concentration camps?"

"Something like that," said Mark lamely.

"What good would that have done?" asked Anna fiercely. "Do you think they would have paid any attention?"

"But she was Hitler's daughter!"

"But no one knew that. Anyway, who listens to kids?" demanded Anna. "Especially not back then. Even today . . ."

She was right, thought Mark. She'd done what she could, even if it was no use at all.

"Maybe it would have been different when she grew up," he said at last. "She could have organized protests then. People would have listened to her if she said she was Hitler's daughter."

"Maybe," said Anna. "But that never happened. There was never any chance of it happening. Because things changed, just a few months later."

"Hey, kids!" It was Mrs. Latter's voice. Mark stared. They'd been so engrossed in the story they hadn't even noticed the bus.

"Thought you'd changed your minds and decided

not to go to school today," joked Mrs. Latter as they climbed on. She was wearing her teapot hat today, the one with the emu embroidered on the front. "What were you all gabbing on about down there?"

"Oh, just things," said Mark. He hated to think what Mrs. Latter would say if she'd heard Anna's story. She'd be on at them about racism and all that.

He glanced at Anna. She sat remote in her seat, not looking at him. She had become quieter ever since she started telling the story, he realized. As though it disturbed her—just like it was disturbing him.

THIRTEEN

DRIP, DRIP, DRIP went the water as it drizzled from the bus shelter roof.

The drips had dug a sort of trench along the edge of the shelter. There was quite a big hole now.

It had become a routine, thought Mark, as he looked at Anna. As soon as she arrived with Little Tracey the story began. He and Little Tracey listened. It was Anna's story, and she'd tell it till it was finished.

How would it end? wondered Mark suddenly. Would it go on and on till Heidi was grown up? Or did she die in the war?

Hitler had killed himself, he remembered, and that woman he married right at the end of the war. Eva Braun, that was her name. They had both killed themselves . . .

No, that couldn't happen to Heidi. It couldn't! Anna couldn't make it end that way!

Anna frowned across the shelter, as though she hunted for the words that would make the story exactly right. Anna could make the story turn out any way she wanted.

Couldn't she?

". . . and she could hear the sounds of planes above the house during the night," Anna continued. "More and more planes came now . . ."

Mark tried to empty his mind. He was missing the story. And anyway he was silly to worry. All of Anna's stories ended happily. Like the one about the disappearing fish and the secret passage under the school.

But this was different.

"That night was different," Anna said. "It was just before they went to bed. Fräulein Gelber had let the fire die down. It was a wood fire, but even wood was getting precious now."

There had been a great stack of wood when they first arrived at the house. Sergeant Amchell was supposed to chop wood for them, but he had been helping with the plowing over at the farm. It was more important than chopping wood, Fräulein Gelber agreed.

Suddenly there was a rumble in the distance. Not a

plane sort of rumble; not even the faint echo of an air raid far away.

"That is a motorbike," Fräulein Gelber said sharply. She went to the door as the motorbike pulled up outside and she opened it before anyone could knock.

Heidi strained her ears to hear. It would have been bad manners for her to go to the door as well. Anyway this might be one of those times when she wasn't supposed to be noticed, as though she didn't exist, had never existed.

Fräulein Gelber closed the door. Her eyes were shining.

"We are to go to meet the Führer," she whispered, as though spies might be listening at the window or round the door. "Quickly! Into your best dress, and your coat, and your good shoes. Hurry!"

A car arrived just as she came down the steps. Like the motorbike, its lights were shaded, so it could not be seen by a plane flying above.

Fräulein Gelber had changed her clothes too. She wore her best hat with the tiny feather. Her hand was trembling as she ushered Heidi through the door and into the car.

She should be excited, Heidi thought, as the car

turned slowly through the gates and began to creep down the lane. It had been, oh, how long had it been since she had seen her father? Over a year, perhaps.

Once she had hoped that he might write her a letter. She had studied hard so she could read it by herself when it came. But no letter had ever come.

Long ago, sometimes there had been phone calls. But there was no phone at the house where they lived now.

She should be excited. But somehow she just felt flat and scared.

The car drove through the village and Heidi looked at it curiously—it was only the second time she had seen it. Frau Leib talked about it so often it was almost as though she knew it. She hoped she might catch a glimpse of the children Frau Leib spoke of. But everyone was indoors.

Past the village, past the church. There was another car pulled up at the side of the road, in the even darker shelter of a tree.

Heidi's car stopped. The driver stepped out and opened their door. Heidi scrambled out first. Fräulein Gelber started to follow her, but the driver shook his head. "Only the child," he said.

It seemed a long way from their car to the other.

Heidi's white socks shone in the moonlight (a tiny moon, a cheese rind of a moon).

The back door of the other car opened. Heidi slid onto the seat.

There was no driver. He must have been told to keep his distance. There was no one to see or hear.

"Well, Heidi," said the Führer, "have you been a good girl?"

"Yes, Duffi," whispered Heidi.

The Führer bent to kiss her on the cheek. His lips were very cold.

"You have been good?" he asked again. It was as though he was thinking of something else, not even hearing when she said "Yes" again.

"Fräulein Gelber has been good to you?"

"Yes, Duffi." It was as if that was all she knew to say. She'd thought of so many things she would say to him—let me come to Berlin, let me help you, look after you, work for you. The words were still in her head. But somehow there was no reason to say any of them now.

"She is also a good girl," said the Führer slowly. "She can be trusted. So few people can be trusted. They are all betraying me. Do you know that, Heidi? All of them! All of them!" His voice rose in the confines of the car.

Heidi shook her head. What should she say? What did he want her to say? "I am still on your side, Father," that's what she ought to say. "You can always trust me."

Heidi was silent.

The Führer looked at her, as though he had just remembered she was there. "You let me know if there is anything you need," he instructed her, though he didn't tell her how. "And you listen to Fräulein Gelber. She can be trusted. But you must always be on your guard."

"Yes, Duffi," said Heidi, for the last time.

"I have to go," said the Führer. "There is so much to do and they will be waiting for me," and Heidi knew then that he hadn't come all this way just to see her.

He kissed her cheek again. She slid along the seat, and out the door and walked back to the other car.

The engine of the Führer's car muttered. The car pulled out onto the road. Heidi watched it as it passed. She lifted her hand to wave, but it was too dark to see if the Führer waved back.

"You are lucky," said Fräulein Gelber, as their car slid back down the lane to home. "With all his other concerns, the Führer still stopped to visit you!"

It was obvious she was bitterly disappointed at not

seeing the Führer too, but she was trying to hide it for Heidi's sake.

For a moment I existed, Heidi thought. But she didn't say the words aloud.

FOURTEEN

"**B**EN'S HERE ALREADY," said Mum, as the car drove up to the bus shelter next morning.

"His cold must be better," said Mark.

Mum nodded. "Remember to keep warm," she said, as though the mention of Ben's cold had reminded her. "There are so many bugs going around. And keep your jacket on at lunchtime."

"Yes, Mum," promised Mark.

"And try not to get your feet wet."

"Mum!" protested Mark. He got out of the car slowly. Blast Ben. Why couldn't he have stayed home just another couple of days?

"Hi," said Ben, blowing on his hands to warm them. "I saw your car from our place, coming down the road, so I raced over here. You're early, aren't you?"

"I suppose so," said Mark. "How are you feeling?"

"Fine. Mum was just stressing out, that was all.

Anything happen while I was sick?"

"Not much. Basketball practice was canceled because of the rain. And old Haskett says we can't have our lunches in the hall if we keep making so much noise."

"Where else would we eat then? Out in the rain?"

"Dunno. Here's Anna." He watched the car drive up and Anna and Little Tracey climb out.

"My auntie Flossy's coming down this weekend," announced Little Tracey, bouncing into the shelter and splattering them both with raindrops as she unbuttoned her raincoat.

"Good for your aunt Flossy," said Ben, wiping his nose with his sleeve. He glanced at his watch. "Everyone's early this morning," he remarked.

"That's because Anna's telling us the story," said Little Tracey.

Ben stared. "You're still playing the Game?"

Anna nodded.

"Yikes. It must be a long story."

Little Tracey nodded. "Come on, Anna!"

"Have there been any good bits?" demanded Ben.

Anna looked at him. "What do you mean, good bits?"

"You know—battles and stuff like that."

Anna didn't reply.

"There've been some bombs," said Mark, then wished he hadn't. It sounded stupid, and both Ben and Anna looked at him like he was dumb.

"Doesn't sound like I've missed much," said Ben, sitting back. He folded his arms, with the hands tucked in to keep them warm.

Anna was still for a moment, then she began to speak.

FIFTEEN

FRÄULEIN GELBER CAME at night. She wore a coat that smelled of foxes, not her dressing-gown. "Heidi! Come on, wake up!"

"What is it?"

"A car has come for us. You must get up now. We have to make a journey."

"To see my father?" It was the first time she had called him that. It had been so long since she had seen him, and what with the dark and sleepiness she had forgotten to call him Duffi.

"Perhaps. Yes. I don't know. Come on, hurry."

Heidi swung her legs out of the bed. "To Berlin?"

Fräulein Gelber nodded. "The car is waiting. Dress warmly. I will pack your bag."

"Are the soldiers coming, Fräulein Gelber?"

Fräulein Gelber didn't look up from the drawers she was emptying. "Yes. They will be here soon."

Both of them knew that she didn't mean German soldiers. The enemy would soon be here. They had to escape before the enemy found them.

"What about Frau Leib?"

Fräulein Gelber shrugged. Frau Leib would have to look after herself, and besides, Heidi realized, she would never leave her family.

"What about my rabbits?"

"Frau Leib will take care of them."

Heidi pulled on her stockings. Thick, woollen stockings. They prickled, but they kept her warm. She glanced around her room at the bright starched curtains, the photographs on the wall. Somehow she knew it was the last time that she would see it.

She left her dolls on the shelf above her bed.

"Come now," said Fräulein Gelber.

Fräulein Gelber's suitcase was in the corner. She picked it up, and handed Heidi hers.

Down the long corridor, down the twisting stairs, along the corridor below and past the kitchen.

"Wait a moment," said Fräulein Gelber.

She quickly packed a basket for the journey with bread and cheese.

But not the sausage, Heidi noticed. Duffi would not

like them to eat the sausage. And she would be seeing Duffi soon.

There were three cars in the driveway, not one. Army cars, with no lights showing. The driver got out of the second car. He took the suitcases and opened the back door. Fräulein Gelber ushered Heidi inside.

The black shadows danced in the moonlight. She could see the shapes of leaves outlined quite clearly on the ground, and the gleam of the moonlight on the frog pond. The frogs were silent.

The first car started its engine and moved off. It did not put its lights on. There was enough light from the moon to see their way.

Their driver started his engine. It spluttered once, and then ran smoothly. They moved after the first car, the third one following behind.

The house was dark behind them.

There was a rug on the seat. Fräulein Gelber spread it over their legs. "It is a very long way to go," she said. "Try to sleep."

"Yes," said Heidi. But she did not close her eyes. She looked out the window instead, at the faint moonlit glimpses of everything passing by.

There was the hedge with the starlings' nests. And

there was Frau Leib's farm, blacker than the moonlit darkness. Even the pigs were asleep, and the baby goat named Heidi.

A plane roared overhead and then another. Fräulein Gelber tensed, and so did Heidi. She hoped it was too dark for the pilots to see them down below, even with the moonlight.

The planes passed overhead. No bombs dropped around them. There was silence, apart from the engines of the cars. Heidi relaxed. For the moment they were safe.

Sometime toward morning she fell asleep, her head on Fräulein Gelber's arm. Fräulein Gelber snored softly beside her, a wisp of spit on one corner of her mouth.

SIXTEEN

THE WALLS OF THE bunker seemed damp, though when Heidi touched them her fingers stayed dry. When she touched the walls she could feel the vibration of the explosions in the world above; the bombs and the tank shells, and other noises too, but Heidi didn't know what they were. Your fingers felt fuzzy if you left them there long enough. It was a game that Heidi played sometimes in the week they'd been in the bunker.

There was not much else to do.

You could hear the explosions too, of course, but it wasn't the same as feeling them. They just went on and on, so you almost got used to them. Then suddenly there would be a louder one than all the others, a high-pitched screaming noise and then the dull thump, thump would start again.

The room was small, concrete and steel deep underground, with a concrete floor. There were double bunks along the side. Heidi had wanted the top bunk, but Fräulein Gelber said, no, she might fall out, and took the top one for herself.

It seemed odd to Heidi that, with the invasion outside, the bombs and rockets and aircraft, Fräulein Gelber was worried that she might fall out of bed. But she said nothing. She was good at saying nothing. She had practiced it all her life.

The room had a wooden table, with a small stove on top and two chairs, and a small alcove curtained off from the rest of the room. Inside the alcove was a basin with two taps, which gave cold water only, and two chamber pots. Fräulein Gelber had to empty the chamber pots into a bucket in the corridor every morning.

A soldier brought in breakfast. There was the end of a loaf of black bread, dusty and hard, not sweet and moist at all, and a piece of cold sausage, and two mugs of imitation coffee, one for her and one for Fräulein Gelber. Even here at the Führer's headquarters food was scarce. Did Duffi know about the sausage? wondered Heidi. Or maybe *any* food was precious now.

Fräulein Gelber divided the sausage and the bread. She hesitated, then she put the bread aside. "For later," she said. The imitation coffee was hot and bitter, the sausage dry and tasteless. Heidi wondered if it was made from horse meat. Frau Leib had told her that that was all they had in the city now.

Fräulein Gelber hadn't remembered to bring any lesson books, and it seemed wrong to sing so far underground. Even talking seemed wrong, with the noise of the explosions, and the hard, worried voices in the corridor outside.

So they sat. Heidi remembered the wind on the lake and the sun on the leaves and all the bright things in the world above. She wondered how much would be left when the planes had dropped their bombs.

A different soldier brought their lunch. It was soup made from potatoes and cabbage; cold, with a thin sheet of fat congealed on the top, so Fräulein Gelber heated it on the stove. The stove warmed up the room, but she turned it off when the soup was hot, as there was not much fuel.

There was bread with the soup, but again Fräulein Gelber put it aside.

It was cold. They had two blankets each on their beds. It was too cold to sit on the chairs so they lay on the bottom bunk together, and Fräulein Gelber wrapped her in all of the blankets, and held her till she slept.

When she woke up Fräulein Gelber had gone. The bread had gone, too. And Fräulein Gelber's suitcase.

Heidi felt no surprise. It was as though she had known it would happen, even though it had never occurred to her it *could* happen.

Of course, Fräulein Gelber would go. She would try to find her family in the mad world up above. Her family might need her, and she would need her family. What was the point of waiting for the soldiers here?

It was lonely in the bunker by herself.

She lay on the bed with the blankets around her till dinner came; more soup and bread and sausage and coffee. There was the same amount as before. No one seemed to have noticed that Fräulein Gelber had left. Or maybe they knew but didn't care.

It took a while to work out how to light the stove. Heidi was scared she'd burn her fingers, but at last she managed it. She drank the soup slowly to make time pass, and then she drank the coffee even though she did not like it. But there was nothing else to do. She took the sausage and the bread back to bed, though she had been told never to eat in bed.

She pretended she was a mouse and could only nibble the food with her front teeth—slowly, slowly,

slowly. Nibble, nibble, nibble. All the while the bombs shattered up above and thudded in the distance, and voices yelled along the corridor.

She slept again, and woke with breakfast. This time she left the door open. It was too lonely with it shut.

People tramped along the corridor, but no one seemed to look inside. No one was interested. Not now.

Suddenly there were louder voices. A man yelled. Another man said something, then the first yelled again. It was a strange yelling—more of a scream than a yell— and it went on and on.

It was her father's voice.

She hadn't seen him since they came to Berlin. He was busy. Of course he was busy. She hadn't even asked where he was.

But he was here.

She slid off the bed, and put the blankets aside. She ran down the corridor toward the voice.

Something shrieked above her. An explosion split the world. Dust fell from the ceiling, or maybe it wasn't dust at all. The bunker rocked, and then was still. She kept on running.

The screaming voice had stopped. But she knew where it had come from.

The door was open. There were three men inside, talking, arguing, their faces white with strain and exhaustion, and from being underground, and other men, soldiers, to the side of the room.

Another explosion shook the air, the ground, the walls.

"Father!" she cried.

It was the first time she had called him father to his face.

The man stopped arguing. He looked at her. His cheeks were sunken. His eyes were dark in darker shadows. There was gray in his moustache.

"Father?" she said again.

The man said nothing. He just smiled at her. Not really a smile—an almost smile. Later she thought it was a smile that said, "Hello, my daughter. Yes, I love you, too. But, for your sake, now I can never say the words."

That's what she hoped, in later years, it might have said.

And then the smile was gone. Maybe there had never really been a smile at all.

"Who is this girl!" demanded the Führer.

"She's . . . she's . . ." one of the guards stammered, and then was silent.

"I have never seen her before," said Adolf Hitler. "What is she doing here? This is no place for a child!"

"But . . ." The guard swallowed what he was going to say. The rest of the room was silent.

"Take her away," said Adolf Hitler. "Now! Do you hear me? Now!"

The guard led her to her room. He shut the door. She sat there trying to listen for her father's voice, but all she could hear now were the bombs.

An hour later, or more perhaps, the guard came again. "Get your suitcase," he ordered.

She picked it up. She expected him to carry it for her, but he didn't.

Along the corridor. The door to the room where her father had been was shut.

Up the stairs, along the next corridor. The noise from the shelling was louder here.

Another soldier waited by the stairs.

"Here she is," said the first.

The second soldier took her suitcase. He was older, and his eyes looked sad. He hesitated, then he took her hand. "Don't be frightened, Mädchen," he said softly. "You are going to good people. Don't be afraid."

The smell was disgusting as they climbed up to the

street. Sweet and strong, like a million chamber pots left too long.

The soldier saw her cover her face with her hand. "They hit the sewers," he told her. "They blew them open . . ."

But that wasn't the whole of the smell.

The world was noise and rubble and splinters of rocks that flew through the air. You could smell the blood and hatred just like you could smell the pigs in Frau Leib's mud.

"This way," said the soldier. He had gray stubble on his cheeks. His voice was tired, and full of tension, but he sounded like he was trying to be kind.

There had once been trees and gardens. Now there was just a battle, too much, too fast to understand.

They ran through the skeleton of the garden, the soldier still holding her hand. Then down some steps, shadowed, down, down, back underground.

Along a tunnel now. The world was quieter, but the ground still shivered under their feet. Along the tunnel, round a corner, along again. There were steps, but they passed them, then more steps, and they climbed those.

It looked like a railway station. She had seen pictures of railway stations. But they hadn't looked quite like this.

They came out of the station. The soldier smoothed her hair. His hand was cold and rough but he was trying to be kind. "They should be here by now. They were supposed to be waiting for you by the . . ."

There was no noise. Or maybe there had been noise but she couldn't hear it in the tumult all around. But suddenly the soldier lay beside her. His arm had been blown off, and red pumped onto the ground. The skin around was very white, and so was the bone. How could a bone be white with so much blood?

She touched his face, but he didn't move.

The world seemed cold and clear and very quiet, in spite of the noise of the bombs.

She had to take her suitcase. She had to leave. She pried it from his hand—his fingers still gripped it even though the arm was half a yard from its body.

Then she began to walk.

She walked for a few seconds, or a few minutes, she didn't know. Then something exploded behind her and reality closed in. She ran for the protection of a rubble wall and crouched there, her suitcase in front of her like a shield.

For some reason she thought of Fräulein Gelber. If only she had saved some bread as Fräulein Gelber had done.

She began to crawl from one wall to another, trying to get as much shelter as she could. With every inch she crawled it seemed she left her old life behind. It was burned out of her by the shells and smoke and fire.

Duffi's daughter was gone. The good girl that Fräulein Gelber had tried to make her be was gone. All that was left was Heidi, a small seed deep inside her.

All she had to do was survive, and that seed could grow.

There were bodies, covered in dust and blood, so that they somehow no longer looked like they were people. There was smoke, drifting in thick pillows; at times it seemed almost solid, and at others just like fog was clouding the world.

The smell was strong and harsh and horrid, like something bad had been cooked a long, long time, but after a while you forgot the smell. The smell and the noise was the way the world was now and it seemed to Heidi impossible that it would ever change.

At first she thought it was only smoke and dust thickening the air. Then she realized it was darkness flowing through the rubble, except where the explosions burned it away.

The noise didn't stop. Nor did it really get dark. There were fires all around now, or perhaps it had just been harder to see the flames in the daylight. The night was red and orange with strange, sharp streaks of white. The air was full of a new sound, a high-pitched squeaking rolling, and the yellow light of flames.

She kept on walking—running—hiding. She didn't know why she ran, or where she was going. There was no time to think now. She just knew that she had to keep on going, to get as far away as possible.

There was a tank in front of her. Two tanks. It was the tanks that had been squealing.

She could hear them rolling grinding up the road even over the noise of the shells. The metal squealed as it hit the stones.

Suddenly, one of the tanks erupted in flames of blue and gray and yellow. The world disappeared below her feet. She fell into the crater and debris rained on top of her, softly it seemed, till she caught her breath, and realized that it hurt.

Her fingers still held her suitcase. She began to crawl out of the crater, away from the flaming ruin of the tank.

"Here! Over here!"

She looked up. A woman was kneeling at the edge of

the crater. The woman held out her hand to Heidi.

Heidi took it. It was cold and smooth.

The hand began to help her up, and suddenly she could move again.

The hand hauled her the final few feet, and then shoved her, safe from the flames and debris, behind a wall.

She looked at her rescuer. She was older than Fräulein Gelber. Or maybe she was younger, and the lines on her face were only signs of strain. A boy stood beside her, a bundle in his arms. He was small—about two or three years younger than she was. His eyes were wide but steady.

"Are you alright?" asked the woman anxiously.

Heidi nodded.

"But there's blood on your face."

"It's not blood. It's a birthmark." Heidi felt her face. Her fingers came away red and damp. There *was* blood, but not very much.

The woman examined her in the fierce yellow pulses of light. "Just scratches, I think," she said. "Where is your mother?"

"I have no mother," said Heidi clearly. "No father either. I'm alone."

The woman was silent for a moment. "Then you must stay with us for now," she said. Her voice was definite, but sort of flat, as though she'd used up all emotion. "We have to get through to the Americans. Away from the Russian soldiers. You understand?"

"The Russians killed Helga," said the boy. They were the first words he'd spoken. His voice was high and fierce.

"Who is Helga?" whispered Heidi.

"My elder sister. They hurt Mutti as well."

The woman beside her began to tremble. She slid down the wall that sheltered them. "We'll rest a minute," she whispered. "Then we'll go on. There is food in the bag if you need it, child."

She closed her eyes.

"Is she alright?" whispered Heidi to the boy.

The boy nodded. "She just needs to rest," he said. "She carried Helga till she died."

His voice was almost matter of fact. He could have been talking about carrying the shopping, unless you looked at his eyes and the white fists of his hands.

"What's your name?" he asked at last.

"Heidi," said Heidi.

"My name is Johannes Wilhem Schmidt," said the

boy. "And my mother is Frau Erna Schmidt and my father is—"

"Is Herr Schmidt," said Heidi.

"His name is Johannes too, like me," said the boy.

"Where is he?"

The boy hesitated. "I don't know. But he'll find us again. Mutti says he will."

"I'm sure he will find you," whispered Heidi.

"You can rest if you like," said Johannes carefully, as another tank squealed by. "I'll look after you."

She almost smiled. He was so small. And so earnest.

"Thank you," she said.

"I'll look after both of you," said Johannes.

Heidi nodded. "I know you will," she said. "And I'll look after you."

SEVENTEEN

THE RAIN SPLUTTERED on the roof, and oozed through the yellow mud along the road. The black-and-white cow opposite took a mouthful of wet grass and munched it sadly. The world was wet and gray and just the same.

"What happened then?" asked Mark finally.

Anna shoved her hands back into her pockets. "Nothing. That's the end of the story."

"But it can't be the end! Please, Anna!" Tracey's small, cold fingers touched her hand.

Anna hesitated.

"Where did she go then? What happened to the Schmidts? Did they escape the Russians? Did they find somewhere safe?" urged Mark.

"Frau Schmidt and Johannes were sent to a refugee camp." Anna's voice was still hesitant. "They got through to the part of Berlin the Americans controlled."

"And Heidi?" urged Mark.

"She went too. Frau Schmidt told the people at the camp that Heidi was her daughter—the one who died. They had to get new papers in the camp, and that's what Heidi's said: Helga Schmidt. She was Helga now."

"And then?"

"And then they came out to Australia." Anna's voice was stronger again.

Mark blinked. "Australia? You mean here!"

Anna nodded.

"But . . . but that's impossible!"

"No, it wasn't! Lots of refugees came here after World War Two. Herr Schmidt found his family in the refugee camp, so they all came out here together. And Herr Schmidt accepted Heidi as his daughter. People had so little then. Just their family. Herr Schmidt said Heidi was '*eine Gabe von Gott*.' A gift from God."

"I didn't know you spoke German," said Mark.

Anna rubbed her cold, red nose. "A few words," she said "Grandma taught me. She spoke a . . . a little German."

Ben frowned. "But Heidi couldn't have come to Australia. We'd have heard if Hitler's daughter came here."

"Dope. She's not real. Remember?" said Mark. But

his voice was uncertain.

"And anyway, no one knew she was Hitler's daughter, did they, Anna?" put in Tracey eagerly.

Anna shook her head.

"Go on," said Mark slowly.

"She went to school in Australia. It took her longer to get through school than for others, because she'd missed so much, and she had to learn English too. Then she went to university. She became a doctor, a pediatrician. That's a doctor for kids," she added for Little Tracey.

"Did she get married?" asked Tracey.

Anna nodded. "She married another doctor, and she had children."

"Hitler's grandchildren!" exclaimed Mark.

"No. Heidi's children," said Anna stubbornly.

"What did her kids do?" asked Ben. "Hey, imagine if one of Hitler's grandkids became Prime Minister. We'd all have to fight him—pow, pow, pow!"

"One became a furniture maker and the other one . . ." Anna hesitated. "I don't know."

"But it's your story!" insisted Mark. "You have to know!"

"A teacher," said Little Tracey firmly. "The other one became a teacher."

Anna half smiled. "Okay. A teacher."

"Cool. Imagine being taught by Hitler's grandkid," remarked Ben. "They'd make you go, *Sieg heil! Sieg heil! Sieg heil!* every morning and you'd have to goosestep into class. I bet he'd have one of those silly moustaches too. Hey, there's the bus! I thought maybe Mrs. Latter had been caught by the floods or something and we'd have to miss school."

The bus pulled up slowly at the verge. Little Tracey ran on first, as she always did. Ben followed more slowly behind. Mark lingered in the bus shelter.

"Anna?"

"Mmm?" Anna picked up her bag.

"Did . . . did Heidi ever tell anyone? About who her father was?"

Anna avoided his eyes. "How could she tell anyone? She'd have been hated, just like her father was hated."

"But it wasn't her fault."

Anna shrugged. "Who'd have believed that? Besides she wanted a new life . . . a real life, like everyone else, with a family and friends to laugh with."

Anna stepped out of the shelter. Mark held her arm, so she had to turn back. "You mean she . . . she just kept quiet? She never told anybody at all?"

Anna nodded. She jerked her arm away, and stepped through the sticky mud and over the gutter, into the cold metallic dampness of the bus.

Mark followed her. He glanced at Little Tracey, in her usual seat behind the driver. She seemed more subdued than usual. Was she, too, thinking of Hitler's daughter, unable to get her from her mind?

Mark sat in the seat behind Anna, as he always did. She was looking out the window, at the wet, sad cows blinking at the bus, the too-green grass limp in their mouths. Her lips were tight and her eyes gleamed silver at the edges.

"Anna?"

"What?" Anna didn't turn around.

"I'm sorry." Mark didn't know why he was apologizing. But it seemed right.

Anna shrugged. Her jacket rustled against the bus seat. Mark tried again.

"Of course I see why she couldn't tell anyone. No one would understand, not really." He tried to put it into words. "She'd be afraid they'd just see Hitler, not her."

Anna turned around and met his eyes. She nodded. "She'd just be Hitler's daughter. All her life . . ."

"I just thought . . ." stumbled Mark, "that maybe . . .

maybe sometimes she couldn't keep it to herself. That she'd have to tell someone . . . just once."

Anna glanced out the window, at the gray sky and grayer rain. Then she looked back at Mark.

"She told her granddaughter," she said softly. "Just once, like you said. One day when it was raining like today. It was just before she died. She told her all about Fräulein Gelber and Frau Leib and the Schmidts. But it was just a story. That's what she told her granddaughter. Only a story. Just pretend, that's all."

"Just pretend," echoed Mark.

Anna nodded. She turned back, and looked out the window again. The wet cows watched them pass in the small, gray bus with orange mud splashed about its wheels, carrying its passengers to school.